D0021437

Mystery in the Whispering Woods

Written by Cathy Hapka
Illustrated by Min Sung Ku

SCHOLASTIC INC.

If you purchased this book without a cover, you should be aware that this book is stolen property. It was reported as "unsold and destroyed" to the publisher, and neither the author nor the publisher has received any payment for this "stripped book."

No part of this publication may be reproduced, stored in a retrieval system, or transmitted in any form or by any means, electronic, mechanical, photocopying, recording, or otherwise, without written permission of the publisher. For information regarding permission, write to Scholastic Inc., Attention: Permissions Department, 557 Broadway, New York, NY 10012.

ISBN 978-0-545-56669-8

LEGO, the LEGO logo and the Brick and Knob configurations are trademarks of the LEGO Group. ©2013 The LEGO Group. Produced by Scholastic Inc. under license from the LEGO Group.

Published by Scholastic Inc. SCHOLASTIC and associated logos are trademarks and/or registered trademarks of Scholastic Inc.

12 11   16 17 18/0

Printed in the U.S.A.   40
First printing, September 2013

Table of Contents

Chapter 1: Mystery Assignment 1

Chapter 2: The Whispering Woods 9

Chapter 3: Camping Surprises 17

Chapter 4: A Spooky Legend 22

Chapter 5: Thumps in the Night 27

Chapter 6: Olivia's New Plan 33

Chapter 7: A Close Call 40

Chapter 8: Catching a Ghost 47

Chapter 9: Heading Home 54

Chapter 1: Mystery Assignment

✳ ✳ ✳

Andrea rushed into the classroom. "Am I late?" she exclaimed.

Her four best friends, Stephanie, Mia, Olivia, and Emma, were gathered around a lab table.

"Don't worry. Ms. Russell isn't even here yet," Stephanie said. "That means you're not late."

"No, it doesn't." Olivia checked the clock. "Class was supposed to start two and a half minutes ago."

Mia rolled her eyes. "You're *so* scientific, Olivia," she teased.

Olivia smiled. "Well, we *are* in science class."

The five friends laughed. It was a crisp fall day at Heartlake High. Outside, the autumn leaves were just beginning to change colors. And this school year, the friends were all in the same science class together. That made everything more fun, because for one thing, they could work in teams on their projects. For another thing, it meant Olivia could help them with their homework!

As they were still chatting, their teacher, Ms. Russell, hurried in. "I'm here, I'm here!" she announced. "Take your seats, please."

"Ms. Russell looks excited," Emma whispered to Andrea. "I hope that doesn't mean we're having a pop quiz today."

"I know, right?" Andrea whispered back. "Ms. Russell *loves* pop quizzes!"

As they were talking, the teacher scribbled big block letters on the whiteboard.

"MYSTERY," Andrea read out loud.

"That's right, Andrea," Ms. Russell said. "Today we're going to talk about mysteries."

"Wait a second," the girls' friend Jacob called out. "I thought this was science class, not English class!"

Everyone laughed, including Ms. Russell. "I'm not talking about the kinds of mysteries that get solved by Sherlock Holmes," she explained. "I'm talking about the mysteries of nature."

Some of the students exchanged confused looks.

mystery

"Can anyone tell me how scientists in the old days figured out what we know about nature today?" Ms. Russell asked.

Olivia raised her hand. "They did experiments?" she guessed.

"That's part of it." Ms. Russell nodded. "But how did they know what to experiment on?"

After a moment, the teacher continued. "Think of it this way. When we see a rainbow in the sky, what causes it?"

Stephanie raised her hand. "Light passing through the water in the air," she answered.

"That's right," Ms. Russell said. "And we know that because we read about it in our textbook earlier this week. But how did scientists first discover what caused a rainbow? How did they decide rainbows weren't caused by, say, magic?"

"Oh, I get it!" Andrea piped up. "Until scientists studied what caused a rainbow, it was a mystery. Something they couldn't explain."

"Exactly." Ms. Russell smiled. "Scientists saw something in nature they didn't understand, and they observed it. For your next group project, I want you to *become* scientists. Find something in the natural world that's a mystery to you. Study it, record your findings, and try to explain it through science."

"But couldn't we just look up the answers on the Internet?" Stephanie asked.

"You could," Ms. Russell replied. "But for this project, I'd like you to act like scientists did before they had the Internet. Once you've observed your mystery, then you can research it online to see if your results are correct. Here's a handout with some guidelines to help you get started."

As Ms. Russell passed out the papers, Stephanie leaned across the table. "We're going to work together, right?" she asked her friends.

"Definitely!" Andrea replied.

"I still don't understand what kind of mystery we're supposed to find," Emma said. "What do you think, Olivia?"

But Olivia didn't answer. She was staring out the classroom window thoughtfully. Suddenly, she snapped her fingers. "I've got it!" she exclaimed. "It's fall, right? Why don't we observe the way leaves change from green to autumn colors?"

"That sounds interesting," Emma said. "I know they change colors when it gets colder. But I've never really thought about why."

Stephanie nodded. "We could go to the park over the weekend and look for evidence."

Olivia smiled. "I've got an even better idea. I'll ask my parents if we can use their camper this weekend. We could camp out in the Whispering Woods— there are lots of autumn leaves there!"

"Fabulous!" Andrea exclaimed.

"Do you think they'll let us use the camper?" Mia asked.

"Why not?" Stephanie shrugged. "We've gone camping lots of times before. Great idea, Olivia! You're a genius!"

"Thanks." Olivia traded a high five with each of her friends. "This is going to be the best science project ever!"

Chapter 2: The Whispering Woods

* * *

Friday afternoon, the autumn sun shone brightly over Heartlake City. Mia looked around the yard as she hurried toward the garden shed.

"We've picked the perfect project," she told her dog, Charlie.

Charlie barked, and then pounced on a pine cone. He picked it up in his mouth.

"Don't eat that!" Mia warned.

She opened the shed and grabbed her family's battery-powered lantern. Then she crossed it off the checklist Olivia had given her of what to pack.

As Mia headed inside, Charlie eagerly followed her. The little dog ran over to the kitchen counter and started barking at a cooler sitting there. It was stuffed with hot dogs, apples, and snacks for the weekend.

"That's not for you." Mia shook her head. "That's people food."

"Almost ready to go, sweetie?" Mia's mom called from the hallway.

"Almost." Mia stuck a package of hot-dog buns in the cooler and snapped it shut. "I just need to finish packing my clothes."

"You'd better hurry." Her mom checked her watch. "Olivia's parents will be here any minute to pick you up."

Mia raced upstairs with Charlie at her heels. Her duffel bag lay open on her bed. The puppy leaped up and sniffed at it.

"Oh, Charlie." Mia giggled. "Those are people *clothes*, and they're still not for you."

A horn honked outside. Mia dashed over to the window. Olivia's gleaming pink and green family camper was parked at the curb.

"Time to go!" Mia said excitedly.

When Mia ran up to the camper, Olivia jumped down from the front seat. "Let me help you put your things in the trailer," she said.

"Thanks!" Mia grinned.

Behind them, Olivia's mom waved from her car. She was going to follow the camper to the woods, and then drive back with Olivia's father once the girls were settled.

As they stowed Mia's things, Olivia suddenly looked down. "Hey, Charlie! Do you want to come with us?"

Mia turned and saw that Charlie had followed her outside. He eagerly wagged his tail.

"Charlie's not allowed to come." Mia laughed. "He'd eat all the mysteries of nature!" She led Charlie back into the house and shut the door.

"Everyone ready?" Olivia asked as Mia came back to the camper.

"You bet," all the friends said together. "It's time to hit the road!"

"Wait!" Mia's mom suddenly rushed out of the house, the front door banging open behind her. She was holding Mia's cooler. "You girls almost forgot to take the food with you!"

"Oops," Mia said. "That would have been bad. Thanks, Mom!"

As Mia strapped herself in, her mom stowed the cooler in the back trailer. Then she waved good-bye and headed back to the house.

"*Now* is everyone ready?" Olivia asked with a bright grin. "Whispering Woods, here we come!"

Soon the camper was rumbling along an unpaved road deep in the forest.

"Let's go over the plan one more time," Olivia said to her friends. "After we set up camp, we'll start collecting leaf samples."

Stephanie nodded. "We'll want to get leaves from lots of different kinds of trees."

"And we'll record the temperature in the woods and how much daylight there is," Emma added. "Those are the two things that change from summer to fall."

"When we get home on Sunday, we can research what we found on the Internet," Mia said. "Ms. Russell said that's okay as long as we observe and come up with a hypothesis ourselves."

Olivia nodded. "I also brought something else to help us."

"What is it?" Andrea asked. "Is it one of your scientific inventions?"

"Maybe." Olivia winked. "But it's a surprise—you'll have to wait and see when we get there."

As the girls rode along, they passed a few other families setting up tents in the woods. Finally, their camper pulled up to a big, flat clearing. A fire pit was in the center, and a large picnic table stood to one side.

"This is great!" Stephanie exclaimed, hopping down to the ground. "We'll have plenty of space to work on our science project here."

"The ranger said we reserved the very last campsite," Olivia explained. "His office is right down the road if we need to use the phone. But otherwise, we'll have this whole area to ourselves."

The friends quickly unpacked and waved good-bye to Olivia's parents. Her dad beeped the horn as they pulled away in her mom's car. Then Olivia turned to the others. There was an excited gleam in her eye.

"Okay," she said. "Is everyone ready to see my surprise?"

Chapter 3:
Camping
Surprises

✳ ✳ ✳

Olivia hurried around to the back of the camper and opened the trailer. She dug something out and held it up. "Ta-da!"

"What is it?" Mia asked. "It looks like a camera with a big extra part on it."

"It is. This camera has a timer," Olivia explained. "I can set it to take a picture every few seconds, every few minutes, or however often I want."

"Cool! Take my picture now." Emma struck a pose. "I worked hard on my camping outfit."

Stephanie laughed. "It's supposed to be for

photographing our mystery of nature, not your fashion sense."

"Well, the way some people dress is a complete mystery to me." Emma waved her hand.

Olivia looked proudly at her invention. "I was thinking we could set up my camera to focus on some leaves," she said. "It will be sort of like a time-lapse film."

"Neat!" Stephanie exclaimed. "Let's go find a good spot to set it up."

"Shouldn't we get our camp ready first?" Emma glanced to the fire pit. "I'm hungry."

"Here." Mia grabbed her cooler from the trailer and pulled out a bag of apples. "We can snack on these while we're setting up our project."

Mia placed the bag on the picnic table and each of the friends grabbed a piece of fruit. They munched as they scouted the nearby woods for the best spot to photograph the autumn leaves. Once the camera was ready, they returned to the camper.

"Hey, who knocked over the apples?" Emma asked.

The girls looked over to where she was pointing. Several apples were scattered across the table and onto the ground.

Mia giggled. "That looks like something Bella would do when she's looking for food."

"It was probably a squirrel," Olivia said. "Come on, let's start the campfire for dinner."

✳ ✳ ✳

"Oof!" Andrea collapsed dramatically onto her sleeping bag. "I'm so full I couldn't eat another bite!"

Night had fallen over the Whispering Woods. The friends had just finished a tasty meal of hot dogs cooked over the fire.

Emma licked mustard off her fingers. "That was delicious. Now what should we do?"

Stephanie rubbed her hands together and grinned. "How about some ghost stories?"

"Ghost stories?" Emma sounded curious.

"I know one!" Andrea leaned forward. "It's called *The Tale of the Phantom Horse*. I remembered it when Mia mentioned Bella earlier."

"You did?" Emma gulped. "Why?"

"Because." Andrea said in a hushed voice. "This ghost story might be *true*!"

***

Emma wrapped both arms around herself and shivered. "Horses aren't scary."

"Real horses aren't," Andrea agreed. "But this is a *ghost* horse. Long ago, when Heartlake City was first founded, the mayor had a beloved horse." Andrea suddenly stopped talking and looked around at each of her friends.

"Well?" Emma said breathlessly.

"Yeah, why'd you stop talking?" Stephanie asked.

Andrea smiled. "Haven't you guys ever heard of a dramatic pause?" Her smile faded, and her voice went dark and spooky again. "Like I was saying, the first mayor of Heartlake City had a very loyal horse. All he had to do was whistle, like this"—Andrea pursed her lips and gave a soft whistle—"and the horse would come galloping over. One day, the horse and his master were on a ride deep in these very woods. Suddenly, they were chased by a pack of hungry wolves!"

"Yikes!" Emma cried, covering her mouth.

Mia looked skeptical. "There are no wolves around here."

"This was a long time ago, remember?" Andrea said. "Anyway, the brave horse galloped as fast as he could to get them to safety. But, suddenly, the path was blocked by a wide, deep river."

"Oh, no!" Olivia exclaimed. "What happened?"

Andrea's voice grew even lower. "The wolves were still coming. There was nowhere to go. So the horse plunged into the rushing river! He tried to make it across—but he got swept away. His master grabbed a floating log and made it to shore. But the loyal horse was lost in the swirling water.

"To this day, whenever the wind whistles through the trees just right," she paused again, making the eerie two-note whistle, "it's said that you can hear the Phantom Horse galloping through these woods in search of his long-lost master."

"Stop!" Emma squeaked. "I'll never be able to sleep tonight!"

"Come on." Mia rolled her eyes. "A ghost horse? That's not very scary. It's not like a ghost shark or crocodile or something."

Olivia shrugged. "The way Andrea told it was pretty scary."

"Yeah," Stephanie agreed. "Andrea is an awesome storyteller!"

"Thank you, thank you." Andrea stood and took a bow as her friends clapped.

Mia stood up, too. She stretched her arms over her head and yawned. "Well, I think that's enough spooky stories for one night," she said. "Let's put out the fire and get ready for bed. We have a lot of science mystery work to do tomorrow, after all!"

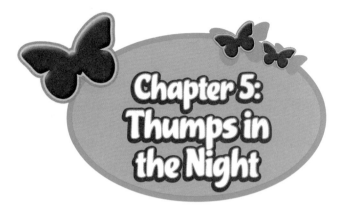

Chapter 5: Thumps in the Night

***

Late that night, Stephanie was dreaming about watching Mia ride her horse, Bella. The horse galloped toward a huge jump. Her hooves thundered.

"Go, Mia. Go, Bella," Stephanie mumbled.

Ka-thump. Ka-thump. Groggily, Stephanie opened her eyes. She thought she had heard something. Had it just been her dream?

KA-THUMP! Now Stephanie shot straight up. It sounded like Bella's hooves had just hit the ground!

"What was that?" Stephanie exclaimed.

Emma's eyes opened. "Steph?" she asked. "Is something wrong?"

"Sorry," Stephanie whispered back. "I thought I heard something."

Emma rubbed her eyes. "What did you hear?"

Stephanie paused. "This is going to sound dumb," she said. "It sounded like a horse's hooves."

"What?" Emma cried.

"Ssh!" Stephanie hissed.

It was too late. The other girls had woken up.

"What's going on?" Andrea mumbled.

"Stephanie said she heard the Phantom Horse!" Emma yelped.

"No, I didn't," Stephanie insisted. "I heard *something*. But I don't know what it was."

Just then, a low whistle sounded in the distance.

"What was that?" Andrea cried.

Emma gasped. "It was the whistle the rider from the legend used to call his Phantom Horse!"

Mia shook her head and yawned. "Come on, guys. We're just getting spooked because of Andrea's story. There's no such thing as ghosts. It's probably an owl or the wind."

The girls remained quiet for a few minutes. But there weren't any other strange sounds.

Stephanie shook her head. "Sorry, guys. I was probably just dreaming." Her eyelids were already starting to droop. "Let's go back to sleep. If we hear anything else, we'll get up and look around."

✱✱✱

By the time Stephanie woke up again, it was morning. Her friends were all still asleep.

"Time to get up!" Stephanie called.

Emma groaned and pulled her pillow over her head. Stephanie nudged her with her toe. "Rise and shine, sleepyhead!"

"I'm hungry." Olivia stretched. "Let's eat."

The girls headed to the trailer. When they reached it, they stopped short.

"Oh, no!" Olivia cried.

The coolers were wide open, the lids knocked aside. All their food was scattered everywhere!

"What happened?" Andrea asked. "How did the coolers get opened?"

Emma gasped. "The ghost ate all our food!" she exclaimed with wide eyes.

"Don't be silly," Mia told her. "Ghosts don't eat food. Besides, it looks like most of it is still here." She bent over and picked up an orange.

"Not all of it." Olivia held up the bag of hot-dog buns. Half of them were gone.

"I'll bet it was the Phantom Horse!" Emma insisted. "It heard us telling its story and didn't like that, so it took our food."

Olivia rolled her eyes. "Emma, come on," she said. "Squirrels and raccoons like food, too." Olivia turned to Stephanie. "Maybe that's what you heard last night—an animal knocking over the cooler. That would explain the thumping noises you heard when you woke up."

"It could be. . . ." Stephanie replied. Her face had gone a bit pale. "But that cooler was closed up tight.

I even put a blanket on top of it so no squirrels or animals would get into it. It's like something *knew* to knock it over. Like something was watching us when we opened it."

Stephanie looked around at her friends, worried. "What if the legend is true?"

Chapter 6: Olivia's New Plan

* * *

Mia couldn't believe her ears. Did her friends actually believe there was a ghost?

"This is silly," Mia insisted. "There's no such thing."

"Are you sure?" Emma asked. "*Something* stole our food last night."

"I heard weird noises," Stephanie added.

"And we *all* heard that spooky whistle!" Andrea exclaimed.

Mia sighed. "That doesn't mean there's a ghost. We just have to figure out what really happened."

"You mean like—a mystery?" Olivia smiled. "Girls, I think we may have found a new science project!"

"What do you mean?" Emma asked.

"We're supposed to explore a mystery of nature, right?" Olivia waved her hand at the trees. "Well, something mysterious is happening out here. We should investigate to figure out what it is!"

Stephanie frowned. "Is researching a ghost allowed?" she asked.

"Let's find out." Olivia ran to the camper and grabbed Ms. Russell's handout. "'Step one,'" she read. "'Find something in nature you don't understand.'"

"Check!" Andrea declared. "We don't understand what is messing with our food and where those strange noises came from."

"'Step two,'" Olivia continued. "'Study the mystery.'"

"We can do that." Stephanie nodded. "We can look for clues like footprints and stuff."

"Don't you mean *hoof*prints?" Emma said.

"'Step three,'" Olivia went on. "'Research the mystery.'"

"We already know the legend of the Phantom Horse," Andrea said. "But we *could* research the history of it. We could see if there's actually a river where the horse would have fallen in. I'm sure the ranger's station will have maps and stuff."

"'Step four: Draw a conclusion,'" Olivia finished. "We can do that once we complete the other steps."

"Then it's settled." Stephanie grinned widely. "Our new project is proving whether or not the Phantom Horse exists!"

"I'll bet no one else in class will be ghost hunting for their project!" Andrea clapped excitedly.

"True." Mia still looked hesitant. "But if this doesn't work, we can still go back to observing the leaves, right?"

The five friends exchanged eager glances.

"Agreed!" they said.

As they ate breakfast, Stephanie worked out a plan.

"Mia, you're our animal expert," she said. "You and I will look for animal footprints around camp."

"Sounds good to me," Mia said.

"Olivia, you'll be in charge of the camera," Stephanie said next.

"Okay." Olivia licked peanut butter off her fingers. "I'll go set it up to take pictures every few minutes. If a wild animal is sneaking in while we're not looking, maybe we can get a photo of it."

Stephanie nodded. "Andrea and Emma, maybe you can walk to the ranger's station and see if they have a map of the woods?"

"Got it," Andrea said. "We can check for rivers like in the legend."

"All right." Stephanie brushed her hands clean. "Time to investigate!"

Stephanie and Mia headed off into the forest while their other friends got to work. They circled the woods near their campsite several times, looking for animal footprints. Mia walked slowly, scanning the ground. Finally, after several laps around, she spotted some fresh paw prints in a muddy patch near the forest trail.

"Stephanie, check this out," Mia called.

Stephanie came running over. "Those look like the paw prints my cat leaves in her litter box," Stephanie said thoughtfully.

"Close." Mia crouched down and pointed. "See how this animal's claws left marks by the toes? That means it's a canine print."

"Like a wolf?" Stephanie asked.

"Or a fox." Mia nodded. "It's about the right size."

"Would a fox steal our food?" Stephanie wondered aloud.

"Maybe." Mia shrugged. "We should take a picture of this print and see if we spot any others like it. Let's go grab Olivia and ask her to bring the cam—"

Mia was cut short by a cry from the clearing.

The two friends looked at one another.

"That sounded like Olivia!" Stephanie exclaimed. "Let's go!"

Chapter 7:
A Close Call

✳ ✳ ✳

Unaware of the excitement back at the campsite, Andrea and Emma were outside the ranger's station studying a map.

"It looks like there should be a creek somewhere over . . . there." Emma pointed out into the woods. "On the map, it seems kind of tiny to be the river from the legend. But let's go look for it, anyway."

The two friends followed the winding forest trail. It twisted and turned deep among thick groves of trees, growing shadier as they went.

"How far is it?" Andrea asked.

Emma checked. "It's hard to tell. This map isn't very detailed." She glanced ahead. "For instance, that fork in the trail isn't on here. I don't know which way we should go."

"Let's split up," Andrea suggested.

Emma looked nervous. "Are you sure? What if we run into the ghost?"

Andrea giggled. "If you get scared, just yell 'help' really loudly, and I'll come right over. I promise." She gave Emma a gentle shove toward the left-hand fork. "Go on. It'll be fine."

As soon as Emma started down her path, Andrea turned to the right. She pushed past low-hanging branches on the trees. It was dim and shadowy in the forest. Dry leaves crunched under her feet.

She continued along the narrow trail, farther and farther away from Emma. Suddenly, a strong gust of wind rushed past. It kicked up the leaves and swirled them around her shoes.

It really is quiet out here, Andrea thought.

Then, very softly, the breeze *whooshed* through the leaves. To Andrea, it sounded like a low, gentle whistle quietly fading away.

"That was weird," Andrea murmured, feeling her heart beat a little faster. The noise didn't sound like the whistle they'd heard the other night. But it didn't sound like the normal wind blowing, either.

Suddenly, something moved in the thick tangle of bushes behind her.

"Emma?" Andrea stammered. "Is that you?"

Andrea spun around, feeling spooked. Her foot slipped off the trail—and into nothingness!

"Help!" Andrea cried loudly. She was slipping down a rocky embankment!

She reached wildly for something to hold onto. Her hand closed around something soft.

Whatever she had grabbed held taut, and Andrea stopped sliding. She dug her heels into the dirt and looked down. She had stumbled upon an empty riverbed in the woods. A small trickle of water ran along the bottom. But at one time, the creek must have been much larger.

"That was close." Andrea sighed in relief.

Then, her heart pounded again. She had been so startled by her fall that she hadn't realized what she was holding was strong but soft . . . kind of like a horse's tail!

Andrea whipped around. Clasped tightly in her fists was a loose, gnarled tree root.

Phew, she thought as she climbed back up. *I'm really letting my imagination get the best of me!* Then, she frowned. *Still, I heard that whistle. . . .*

Just then, Emma came rushing toward her. "What happened?" she asked. "I heard you scream."

"I slipped," Andrea said, her voice shaky. "I almost fell into that." She pointed down into the rocky gully.

"Whoa." Emma followed her gaze. "Is *that* the creek?" She glanced at the map and back into the empty gully. "Now I get why the water is so small on the map. The bed is all dried up. Andrea, I think you found our legendary river!" Then she looked at her friend. "Are you okay? You didn't get hurt, did you?"

"No, I'm all right." Andrea breathed. "I grabbed onto this." She pointed to the tree root. "But I thought I heard something, just before I fell."

"Like what?" Emma asked.

"A whistle, high up in the trees," Andrea replied slowly. "For a moment, I could have sworn . . ."

Andrea gazed at the root for a long while. Finally, she looked back up at Emma. "Are you sure you didn't hear anything?" she asked.

Emma shook her head. "Now *you're* starting to creep me out," she said. "I didn't hear anything. Only you when you called for help."

Andrea looked back down at the rocky creek bed and shivered. "Let's head back to camp and see what the others have found," she said. "I don't think we should stay here longer than we have to."

Chapter 8: Catching A Ghost

✳ ✳ ✳

Back at the campsite, Mia and Stephanie raced toward Olivia. Their friend was on her knees by the picnic table.

"Olivia, are you okay?" Mia exclaimed.

"What happened?" Stephanie asked urgently.

Olivia looked up. "I'm okay," she said. "But my camera's not. Look."

She held out the camera she had modified so her friends could see. The special timer attached to the top was completely broken.

"The picture memory card was full, so I went

into the camper to get a new one," Olivia explained. "When I came out, something had knocked the camera over. The timer is ruined. It's like something didn't *want* us taking pictures of it."

"Like the Phantom Horse!" Stephanie exclaimed.

"Let me see," Mia said, reaching out. She turned the camera over in her hands. "*Ew*—it's slimy!"

Stephanie cautiously touched the camera. "Yuck. You're right. It's wet—like ghost slime!"

"Or animal drool," Mia added. "Let's check for pictures."

Olivia scrolled through all the photos on the camera. "I don't see anything—wait! Here's one!"

Stephanie and Mia peered over Olivia's shoulder.

"Is that . . . a tongue?" Stephanie asked.

"It's a little hard to tell," Olivia said. "Does it look like a tongue to you, Mia?"

Mia didn't reply.

"Mia?" Stephanie asked.

With a shake, Mia snapped out of it. "Yeah," she said. "It's just, that picture gives me an idea." She looked at her friends and smiled. "Guys, I think I know how we can solve our mystery!"

✳✳✳

As Stephanie, Mia, and Olivia were working at the picnic table, Emma and Andrea raced up to the campsite. "Guys, you'll never believe what happened," Emma shouted. "The Phantom Horse saved Andrea!"

"The Phantom Horse did what?" Mia asked.

Emma quickly explained what had happened.

"Are you okay, A?" Mia asked, concerned. "You could have gotten hurt."

Andrea nodded. "I'm fine. And I don't know for sure the Phantom Horse saved me." She rolled her eyes at Emma. "But something really weird is going on. Did you guys find any other clues?"

Mia, Olivia, and Stephanie exchanged a look.

"Actually," Olivia said, "Mia has a plan to prove that there *isn't* a ghost after all."

"You do?" Emma and Andrea asked together.

Mia nodded. "Whoever or *whatever* the culprit is left a clue on Olivia's camera." She pointed to the slimy box. "And it gave me an idea. We're almost set up here. Andrea, if you wouldn't mind grabbing the cooler, we'll put the last pieces into place and catch our 'ghost' once and for all."

✳ ✳ ✳

As the sun was starting to set, the girls put their new plan into action. "Places, everyone!" Stephanie whispered.

Mia set a plate of hot dogs on the picnic table beside Olivia's camera, and then hurried out of sight around the camper. Olivia hid behind a large tree trunk. She held a small remote in her hand that had come with camera. It would let her snap pictures from a distance.

Nearby, Emma crouched next to a large rock. Stephanie and Andrea joined Mia behind the camper. All five girls had chosen spots where they could see the whole clearing.

"Do you think this will work?" Andrea whispered.

"I hope so," Mia whispered back. She pursed her lips and whistled: *"Whooooo!"*

There was silence. Mia held her breath.

If the legend were true, that whistle should attract the Phantom Horse.

Nothing happened. After a moment, Andrea leaned closer.

"Try it again," she whispered.

"*Whooooo!*" Mia whistled.

It grew darker and darker in the clearing as Mia continued to whistle.

Soon the only light came from the campfire.

"*Whooooo!*" Mia whistled a final time.

Suddenly, the quiet was broken by loud rustling in the bushes nearby.

"Look!" Andrea whispered. "Something's coming!"

Mia leaned forward and held her breath. A shadowy figure was creeping out of the woods!

Chapter 9:
Heading Home

✳ ✳ ✳

Olivia jumped out from behind the tree and started snapping pictures as fast as she could. "I got it!" she cried. "I got its picture!"

"It's the ghost horse!" Andrea exclaimed. "Quick! Grab it!"

"That might be a ghost, but it's no horse." Mia rushed out and switched on her flashlight.

Instantly, the clearing was bathed in bright, white light. A small figure crouched by the picnic table, blinking at them.

Mia gasped. The creature looked awfully familiar.

"*Charlie?*" Mia cried. "What are you doing here?"

At the sound of her voice, the little dog wagged his tail. He barked and leaped onto the picnic table—straight for the hot dogs!

Andrea burst out laughing. "It *is* Charlie!"

Mia grabbed the puppy in a hug. "How did you get out?" she asked. "I shut the door before I left."

Olivia thought back to the previous day. "Wait, didn't your mom come out after you?" she asked.

Mia's eyes grew wide. "You're right! He must have sneaked back out when she opened the door."

"But how did he get all the way up here?" Emma asked. "Did he follow the camper? Or maybe he stowed away in the trailer?"

"Of course." Mia smacked her head with her hand. "He went after the cooler! He saw me put the hot dogs in. He's always trying to pop the lid off."

"But why haven't we seen him?" Olivia asked.

"I don't know." Mia shrugged as Charlie licked her face. "That part is still a mystery."

Suddenly, a loud whistle pierced through the darkness. Everyone froze.

"Did you hear that?" Emma squeaked.

"Here, boy!" a voice called.

"Where'd you go?" another voice shouted.

A moment later, a man and a young boy with flashlights stepped into the clearing.

"Oh, hello," the man said. "Sorry to bother you. My son and I are looking for a lost puppy." He smiled when he spotted Charlie in Mia's arms. "Hey, that's him right there!"

"Actually, this is my puppy, Charlie," Mia said. "He came camping with us by accident."

"Oh, that explains it!" The man laughed. "That fella sure has an appetite. He came sniffing by our tent last night. We thought he was a stray."

"We've been feeding him!" the young boy chimed in. "He really likes hot dogs."

Mia shook her head. "So *that's* where you've been going." She ruffled Charlie's fur. "You followed your stomach!"

"Well, I'm glad he has an owner," the man chuckled. "At least he's safe and sound now."

The girls thanked the two campers for taking care of Charlie. Then the father and son headed away.

"Silly Charlie," Andrea said. "You made us think you were a ghost horse."

"That's why we kept hearing whistles," Olivia realized. "It was that man calling for Charlie when he wandered off."

"I *told* you guys there was no ghost horse," Mia said. "All our evidence points to Charlie."

"Well, not quite *all* of it," Emma said. "Why did Charlie drool on the camera?"

Mia grinned. "Actually, that's what gave me the idea for our experiment. I noticed Olivia licking peanut butter off her fingers right before she went to set up the camera. When I saw there was drool on it, and the picture of the tongue, I figured all we had to do was set up more bait, and our thief would come."

Olivia nodded. "It was a hungry little dog the whole time."

"But what about what happened to Andrea in the woods?" Emma insisted. "She said the whistle she heard didn't sound like the others."

All four girls looked at Andrea.

After a moment, Andrea shrugged. "It must have just been the wind," she said finally. "And I was lucky that the root was there."

"Yeah," Stephanie agreed. "You could have really gotten hurt. No more wandering off for any of us." She rubbed Charlie's belly. "That includes you, you hungry puppy."

Charlie barked. All the friends laughed.

✳✳✳

By the next morning, the girls had fully planned their project presentation.

"When we get home, we'll shoot some video of Andrea telling *The Tale of the Phantom Horse,*" Stephanie said as she rolled up her sleeping bag.

Olivia nodded. "I have pictures of Charlie, his paw prints, and the spilled food. We can use them to explain how we searched for clues and how Mia came up with her experiment."

"Sounds good." Stephanie brushed off her hands and looked around. Everything was packed away. "This was great, wasn't it?"

"Definitely." Emma grinned. "I wish *all* our homework was this much fun!"

Just then, a car horn beeped. Olivia's parents pulled up to the clearing. "Did you have a good time?" Olivia's dad asked as he hopped out.

"The best!" all five of them replied.

Mia, Emma, Stephanie, and Olivia clambered

into the camper. But Andrea hung back. She glanced over her shoulder, out at the trees. The wind rustled past, swirling the leaves across the ground.

"Thank you," she said very quietly.

"Everything okay, A?" Olivia poked her head back out of the camper.

Andrea turned. "Yeah," she said with a smile. "Let's go home."